THE KITCHEN WARRIORS

The elves' village is in the china-cupboard, behind
the soup bowls and the sugar basin and the pile of
bread-and-butter plates. Of course THEY – the
people who live in the house – can't see it; in fact the
village is not visible at all by daylight. But in the
dark it glows, and that is when the elves go about
their business.

The same kitchen is also the home of Fendire, the
Infra-red dragon; the deep-freeze trolls, who can
swallow an elf at a mouthful; the slimy, hungry,
terribly strong evil kelpies in the dishwasher, Norn
of the broom-cupboard, the dog Garm and Mistigris
the cat.

All these provide dangerous adventures for young
Prince Coriander, returned home at last following
his education by the Garden Elves.

Joan Aiken has conjured up an enchantingly
magical world which will delight all young children
of six and over.

THE KITCHEN
WARRIORS

Joan Aiken

Illustrated by Jo Worth

AS TOLD IN JACKANORY

BBC/KNIGHT

Copyright © Joan Aiken Enterprises Ltd 1983
Illustrations © British Broadcasting Corporation 1983
First published 1983 by the British Broadcasting Corporation/Knight Books

British Library C.I.P.

Aiken, Joan
  The kitchen warriors.
  I. Title
  823'.914[J]   PZ7

ISBN 0-340-33517 3

(ISBN 0-563-20217 3 BBC)

Printed and bound in Great Britain for the British Broadcasting Corporation, 35 Marylebone High Street, London W1M 4AA and Hodder and Stoughton Paperbacks, a division of Hodder and Stoughton Ltd., Mill Road, Dunton Green, Sevenoaks, Kent (Editorial Office: 47 Bedford Square, London, WC1 3DP) by Cox and Wyman Ltd., Reading.

Contents

1   Prince Coriander's Return

The King of the Elves had lost his crown. It was a very old and beautiful one, which had been in the royal family for thousands of years. Also, without having his crown on his head, the king would not be able to make laws, or eat his breakfast, or see ambassadors, or die, or give judgments at the Royal Elvish Games.

So everybody in the elves' village was in a terrible state of worry and confusion, dashing hither and thither, moving furniture, pulling down curtains, digging, and pushing one another out of the way.

The elves' village is in the china-cupboard, behind the soup bowls and the sugar basin and the pile of bread-and-butter plates. Of course THEY – the people who live in the house – can't see it; in fact the village is not visible at all by daylight. But in the dark it glows, and that is when the elves go about their business.

THEY – the people who live in the house – had been spring-cleaning; all the china had been taken out of the cupboard, and the cups and plates and bowls washed and then put back again. That, the king said, was when the crown must have been lost.

He was scolding all his subjects. "The crown should have been put away in my treasure chest!" he stormed. "We heard THEM talking about spring-cleaning last week. Why did nobody take proper care of the crown?"

"But Corodil," said his wife the queen, with tears in her eyes, "you were wearing the crown yourself until late last night, just before you went to bed. How could anybody put it in the treasure chest? Can't you remember what you did with it when you took it off to go to bed?"

"I did just what I always do with it!" snapped King Corodil.

But the trouble was that he did something different with his crown every night. Sometimes he hung it on a cup-hook with the best after-dinner coffee-cups. Sometimes he climbed out of the china-cupboard and hid the crown inside the butter-dish in the refrigerator. Sometimes he went into the pantry, and stowed the crown among the onions or potatoes.

The crown might be almost anywhere, and the poor elves were wearing themselves out, searching here and there all over the kitchen. They had to be extremely careful and quiet, and look sharply about

them as they did this, for the kitchen is full of dangers. There is Fendire, the Infra-red dragon, who generally lurks behind the gas burners but may come roaring out any minute, with red-hot eyes and tongue. There are the deep-freeze trolls, blazing blue, who can swallow an elf at a mouthful, or turn a whole regiment of elves into ice-powder. There are the evil kelpies in the dishwasher, who are slimy and hungry and terribly strong. There is the Norn of the broom-cupboard, who sometimes comes out riding on her three-legged broom, and is capable of grabbing handfuls of elves in her sharp talons. There is the dog Garm, who sleeps in front of the coal stove, and the cat Mistigris, whose basket is under the kitchen table.

All these perils had to be faced by the searching elves. But the elves did face them bravely, hunting far and wide, all over the kitchen, while King Corodil grumbled and fumed and urged them to make haste. He was hungry and wanted his breakfast of bread and honey and a golden cup of warm mead. But, of course, by elf law, without his crown on his head, he might not eat or drink or do anything at all, except grumble.

"Well, Corodil," said Queen Corasin, "you might at least brush your teeth and comb your hair and beard, while you are waiting for them to find the crown."

These things were allowed. But the king said, "I shall do nothing of the sort!" His white hair and cloudy beard were so long and woolly and tangly that he looked like a bundle of dandelion clocks. "I shall do nothing at all but sit on my throne until the crown is found," he said, and folded his arms.

In the middle of all the commotion, a stranger arrived at the elf palace. This was a handsome young man, who looked like an elf prince. He wore a sword, and was well dressed, but seemed to have come from a long way off, for he looked tired, and his clothes were much stained with travel, as if he had been on boats, and swum across rivers, and climbed mountains, and pushed his way through forests. As indeed he had.

"Who are *you*?" growled King Corodil, eyeing the young man without favour. "And where have you come from?"

"I'm your son Coriander. Don't you recognise me? You sent me away at age three, to be educated among the Garden Elves. Now I'm of age, so I have come home."

Queen Corasin cried, "Oh, my dear, dear son! How delighted I am that you have come home at last!"

But King Corodil muttered, "I don't recognise you. How can we be sure that you are my son?"

"Here is the sword that you left for me," replied Prince Coriander, and he pulled the sword from its scabbard. The blade was all inscribed with runes, and the silver-mounted handle set with sapphires.

"It *looks* like the sword," said the King, "but how

do I know you didn't pinch it from some other fellow, eh?"

"Oh, Corodil," cried his wife, "don't you see that the prince is the very spit image of what *you* looked like when you were that age? *Anybody* could see that." And she gave the young man a hug, and he gave her one back.

But King Corodil, who was becoming hungrier and hungrier, and angrier and angrier, exclaimed, "If you are really my son, the best way you can prove it is to find my crown, which some dumb mutton-headed fool seems to have lost. You find the crown, so that I can eat my breakfast, and then we'll see about recognising you, and all that business."

"Very well," said Prince Coriander, "though it's a poor way of greeting your only son when he comes back to the palace after eighteen years. Where is the crown most likely to be?"

"That's just what nobody knows!"

Prince Coriander began to search. First he went into the dark pantry, which smelt of onions and apples. A terrible growl came from the huge dog Garm as he passed its basket in front of the coal stove, but the brave prince pulled out a silver whistle and blew it so piercingly in the dog's ear that Garm sank down again, and hid his head between his paws.

Prince Coriander searched all through the pantry, but the crown was not there; or at least he did not find it. He returned to the kitchen, passing the

broom-cupboard on his way. A whiff of cold, dark, stale air came out under the door, and he heard the hiss of the Norn, stirring in her cobwebby corner.

But the Queen had said, "Your dear father *never* goes into the broom-cupboard, so don't look there."

Prince Coriander scrambled up and looked down into the sink. There were the nixies, beautiful green sisters with long silky hair. They were making a ladder of their hair to climb up to the taps, and turning them on, and sliding down the long twisted rope of water that came out.

"Hey, you nixies! Have you seen my father's crown?" he called to them, and they laughed and said, "If we had, handsome prince, do you think that we would tell you?"

14

"Yes!" he called, and tossed them an ivory rose.

They had never seen such a thing, and shrieked with joy.

"For that, beautiful prince," said the eldest nixie sister, putting the rose in her hair, "we will tell you that your father's crown is not here. And it is not among the trolls, either, for our youngest sister Waterslenda has been captured by the trolls, and cries to us daily to set her free. If the crown were there, she would have seen it. Nor is it in the dishwasher, where the kelpies live, for if it were there we should certainly know. Perhaps the crown has been taken by the Vacuum witch. You had better ask her."

"Where is she to be found?"

"In the Utility Desert, a long journey from here. But the dangers are terrible. You had much better stay here and play with us."

"No, I can't do that just now," said Prince Coriander, "for I have promised to find my father's crown. But when I have done that, I will try to rescue your sister from the trolls."

"Take care, then! For the witch can swallow you at a gulp! You need to arm yourself with a long, long spear, and hold it crossways, so that she will not be able to bite you. Wait, and we will give you one."

The prince thought this sounded like useful advice. The nixies, who have power over all shining things, gave him a slender spear that was made of diamond from end to end, clear as water, harder than steel, and it shone like a lamp, too, giving him light in the Utility Desert, which was a dark, grim place, dusty and cold and so huge that it would take an elf ten days to cross it. But luckily the Vacuum witch lived on the near side.

She was coiled up, hanging from a hook like a huge snake with batwings, and she opened her jaws wide as Prince Coriander approached. But he held his glowing spear crossways, and, while she was turning her horrid head this way and that, wondering how she could manage to swallow him, he called out: "Hey, you Vacuum witch! Have you swallowed my father's crown? For, let me tell you this: that crown was made from ninety different red-hot metals in the workshop at the centre of the earth, and, if you have swallowed it, the spells engraved inside the crown foretell that you will have indigestion for ninety times ninety years."

"Well, I *do get* a bit of indigestion, as a matter of fact," mumbled the witch. "I've been wondering what caused it."

"Try a bit of this," said the prince, and he tossed her a flower of elvish mint which he had brought with him from the Garden Elves.

The witch gulped down the flower, waited a few minutes, and then said, "That has cured my heartburn. For which, I thank you! But just the same, that won't stop me from swallowing you, the minute you drop your spear!" and she opened her wide jaws again.

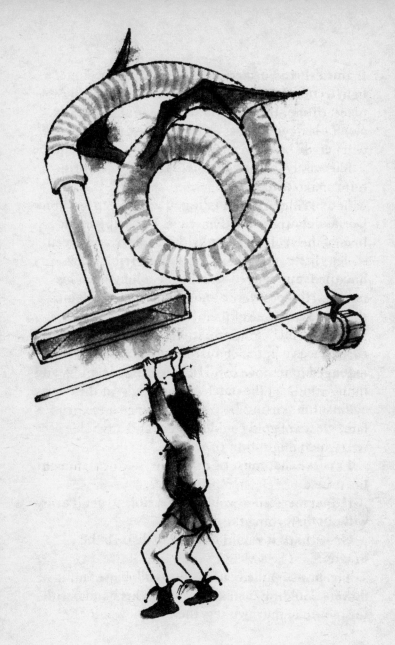

But Prince Coriander had already leaped out of reach, crying, "Ho, no, witch, you won't swallow me this time. If the flower can cure you, then you cannot have my father's crown inside you."

"Very likely the Infra-red dragon has it," said the witch sulkily, closing her jaws again, as the prince returned to the kitchen.

Fendire the Infra-red dragon was asleep as Prince Coriander approached his cave. High up, on the bars of the grill, he hung, with his black and green scales glistening greasily, and his horrible claws uncurled, and his red-hot tongue lolling from his mouth. His eyes were almost shut, all but a faint spark of fire in one of them.

A long way below him, underneath the gas cooker, was a patch of dust which THEY had not managed to remove in THEIR spring-cleaning, and in the middle of the patch of dust, right at the back, against the skirting-board, something shone – just a faint gleam of gold could be seen, and a twinkle of red, which might be a ruby.

I believe that must be my father's crown, thought the prince.

He wondered if it would be possible to get it away without disturbing the dragon.

Or perhaps it would be *better* to disturb the dragon?

The prince pulled out his little silk bag of mint flowers. Holding the bag cupped in his hands, with the mouth of it drawn together, he blew into the

narrow mouth – blew and blew and blew, until the bag swelled up like a balloon, to the size of the prince's head. Then, still holding the mouth twisted together with his teeth, to prevent the air escaping, he clapped his hands against the sides of the bag, so that it exploded with a violent bang.

The dragon woke with a start. Mint flowers were whirling all round his head. He sneezed and sneezed and sneezed again, and, still sneezing, dropped to the floor. There he saw Prince Coriander, and rushed at him with a roar, darting out tongues of flame in every direction. But halfway through his charge he had to stop and sneeze again, and, while he was doing that, the prince dashed underneath the gas cooker, grabbed the little gold shining dusty object, and sprang way again.

But the dragon went roaring after him, hissing and flaming and spitting out red-hot grease. The prince turned boldly, with his long diamond spear braced to receive the dragon's charge. Whether it would have killed the dragon, who can say? But at that same moment, the dragon let out a wail.

"My handkerchief! My enchanted rag! I had it tucked down behind the grill, and it has blown out of the window. Oh, I must find it at once, at once, for if it is lost for a year and a day I shall grow cold and die, oh, oh, oh, oh!"

And, whirling and flaming, he rushed away to look for his enchanted handkerchief.

Prince Coriander lost not an instant in leaping up

on to the kitchen table, on to the counter, on to the bread bin, and so up into the china-cupboard and back to safety.

"Look, father!" he called, as he strode into the elves' village. "Look, I have found your crown!"

For the object that he had found, though dusty and greasy, was, indubitably, a very beautiful, ancient crown, made from ninety-nine different metals, and ninety-nine different jewels, with a

different spell carved on each precious stone and a different rune inscribed on each strip of metal.

But King Corodil looked on the crown with great suspicion.

"That? *That*'s not my crown! That's the crown of my great-great-grandfather Corasinny, which was lost a thousand years ago. I remember the description of it, and all the fuss when it was lost."

"Well, but, Corodil dear," said his patient wife, "it will do, won't it? It's a crown, after all. You can put it on and eat your breakfast."

"That's true," said Corodil, brightening.

"Just let me comb your beard a little first." So she began to comb his beard saying, "Now that our dear son Coriander has come home we must summon all the elves together and hold a feast – oh!"

For as she combed his beard, what should tumble out of it but his very own crown, which had become tangled up and lost in there while he slept.

"*That*'s my *proper* crown," said King Corodil with relief. "Now I can have breakfast and be born and die and make laws and judge the Elvish Games. You had better hang that other crown up somewhere. It might come in useful to have a spare."

So the ancient crown was hung on a cup-hook, and all the elves came to the palace for a feast, to celebrate the homecoming of Prince Coriander. They sang and laughed and ate and drank all night, until the sun rose, and THEY came down for the day.

2   The Cat Mistigris

The Royal Elvish Games were being held in honour
of Prince Coriander's return to his father's palace.
On the kitchen floor at night (after THEY had gone
to bed) there were chariot races, round and round
the kitchen table. And there were horse races, which
took place in the space between the great dog Garm
and the deep-freeze. The dog Garm had been given
an enormous honey-cake, baked in the palace
bakery and spiced with poppy seed; it had sent him
into a deep sleep from which it was to be hoped he
would not wake for nine hours; so that it was safe to
start the horse races from a point just two inches
beyond his tail. A similar honey-cake would have
been given to the cat, Mistigris, but for two reasons:
the cat Mistigris didn't like honey-cakes, and also he
was out at the time the Games began. In fact the cat
Mistigris often stayed out all night, and the elves
hoped he would do so tonight.

Running races were held on the floor space between the sink and the broom-cupboard. Elves are extremely fast runners. They have to be, for there are so many dangers they must run from. And, though people don't realise this, the kitchen elves have very little magic about them. They can make themselves invisible for short periods, in emergency, but it is hard work, like holding your breath, and soon wears off. They can jump tremendously high – they have the same power of take-off as a grasshopper, which often saves them in danger – but this knack, too, may desert them when they are tired or upset. In daylight, the elves are invisible to people – except just a very few with sharp eyesight – but they are visible to cats, dogs, and birds.

After the high-jump events, chariot races, horse races, and running races, wreaths of laurel tied with golden ribbons were handed out to the winners. There were no other prizes. These wreaths were considered a terrific honour, and the prize-winners wore them for months, until they dropped to bits.

After this prize-giving, a good deal of mead was drunk, before the next events were due to begin: the long jump, discus throwing, and wrestling.

A couple of hundred-inch winners, Hirondel and Dibdin, became rather lively on mead, and they began to boast. "It's just as well the cat Mistigris isn't here," said Hirondel, "for if he was, I'd climb up his fur and pull out his whiskers."

"It certainly is a good thing he isn't here," said

Dibdin, "for if he were sitting under the kitchen table, I'd tie his whiskers into a granny knot."

"I'd fill his ears with cobwebs, so that he couldn't hear us."

"I'd bandage his eyes with mushroom peel, so that he couldn't see us."

"Oh, be quiet, you silly fellows," said their girl friends Ilthra and Chraselas. "You've both had much too much to drink and you are talking a pack of rubbish."

But the two winners took no notice of this sensible advice.

"I tell you what I'd do," said Hirondel. "If the cat Mistigris came in now, I'd rig up a sling out of a teacloth, and I'd fix a crane and tackle under the kitchen table, and I'd hoist Mistigris into the air, so

27

that he just hung there dangling, and didn't interrupt our Games."

As it happened, King Corodil, who had a seat right in front of the stands, for he was the judge and umpire of the Games, heard these boastful words.

"Oh you would, would you?" he said rather sharply, for he was an elderly man, and the Games had been going on for several hours by now, and his feet hurt, and his crown was fidgeting him, and he wanted to have his supper and take off the crown and go to bed. "Well, if the cat Mistigris does come in, you can just *do* that; otherwise you shall be exiled for a hundred years."

At this a general hiss of horror went up from the elves; for of course the Elf King's word is law, if he has his crown on, and even he himself can't go back on it. Hirondel turned quite pale, but he said stoutly, "Of course I should be glad to do it, your majesty – if the cat Mistigris *should* chance to come in."

Just at that moment the cat Mistigris did come in, through his cat-flap. It had started to rain rather heavily, and his fur was all wet; he wanted to warm up and dry off.

All the elves shot into the air like grasshoppers. Most of them landed on the kitchen table. Some hurried into the china-cupboard, where their village was, behind the soup bowls.

King Corodil, stroking his long white beard and settling his crown more firmly on his head, said, with great briskness: "Well, Hirondel! Now it's up to you! Sling up the cat – otherwise you are due for a hundred years' exile."

Poor Hirondel turned white as the table cloth. Elf years are not so long as human years – but just the same a dismal prospect lay ahead of him. Nor did he have the least notion in the world how to rig up a crane and sling and hoist the cat Mistigris into the air. But he gulped and said, "Yes sir, naturally I'll do my best."

His girl friend Ilthra gave his hand a squeeze and said, "I'll help you." And so did his friend Dibdin, who had in fact begun the boasting and felt rather bad about it. Dibdin's girl friend Chraselas also offered to help. So the four of them sat on the edge of the kitchen table, with their legs dangling, and thought hard, while, on the black-and-white tiled floor below them, the cat Mistigris, who was grey all over, began to wash the wet off himself with his rough pink tongue. Mistigris took no notice of the elves so long as they didn't interfere with him. He knew they were not very good to eat. He preferred mice; or tins of Kittigoo.

Mistigris leaned over backwards, propping himself on his two front legs, and stuck up a back foot in the air like a leg of mutton. Then he started work on licking it dry and clean.

"First we need a teacloth," said Dibdin.

"I can get that," said Ilthra. She was a marvellous jumper and had won a laurel wreath in the high-jump event. She sprang up in the air to where the teacloths hung on the Dutch airer, tweaked one loose, and returned to the kitchen table, with the teacloth falling down behind her like half the sky.

"Now, we need a lot of rope," said Chraselas.

Rope was soon produced. The elves make it out of twisted human hair, which they find on carpets. The hair is soaked in hippocras, and doubled and plaited and twisted; it makes a particularly strong rope.

"Now we need a hook," said Ilthra.

Dibdin knew where a cup-hook had been left by one of THEM at the back of the china-cupboard; it lay behind a pile of saucers. He went and fetched it. It was too heavy for him to carry without help, so Prince Coriander came to his aid. The prince had been longing to do something for the four friends, since the Games were being held in his honour. He felt sad about this upsetting incident, and very sorry that King Corodil had lost his temper.

The hook was lowered by a long rope from the china-cupboard to the kitchen table.

"Now we have to screw it into the underside of the kitchen table," said Dibdin. "How in the world are we going to do that?"

Another friend, Chanterol, who was a noted climber, volunteered to screw in the hook. He descended the table leg, driving in little tiny sharp pegs at each step to make holds for his feet; then he climbed up inside under the table top, using the same method. He took with him a high-speed drill, made from wasps' teeth, with which he rapidly bored a hole in the underside of the table. The cup-hook, slung on a rope which passed from side to side of the table, was then lowered down, and he pulled it along until it dangled just beneath the hole he had bored.

Then the two girls, who were both expert tightrope walkers, approached the hook from each end of the rope, turned it the other way up, and helped Chanterol screw it into the hole he had bored.

Now the rope was attached to the hook and hung down to the ground, dangling beside the cat Mistigris, who took no notice of it at all. Mistigris had dried off both hind legs and was hard at work on his ears, rubbing them with the back of his front paws.

"Now we have to fasten the teacloth to the rope," said Hirondel. "Who ties the best knots?"

Prince Coriander did. While he was away, learning the trade of a prince with the Garden Elves, he had spent a year in the navy, sailing about on the garden pond in ships made of walnut shells. He and Hirondel descended to ground level and fastened one corner of the teacloth to the end of the rope. Then they stood scratching their heads, looking at the cat Mistigris, who towered above them like an elephant.

"How are we going to get the teacloth underneath him?" said Coriander.

"If we could just make him stand up for a moment," said Hirondel, "I could run through from one side to the other carrying the end of the cloth that's tied to the rope. Then, even if he sat down again, we might all be able to pull it through."

"If we bother him too much, he might bite us."

This was true. Mistigris had a hasty temper and didn't care to be touched. He had been known to do bad damage to elves who accidentally got in his way.

"He is not going to like this," said Chanterol, who had joined them.

"No he isn't," said Ilthra. She sounded very worried.

"I'll run through under his stomach," said Dibdin bravely. "It was my fault all this got started."

"Perhaps if we peeled an onion close beside him, he would stand up," said Chraselas. "Mistigris hates the smell of onion."

She went to the pantry and found a small onion. Ilthra helped her strip off the skin; then, with an axe, they hacked the onion in half. All the elves in

the kitchen began to stream with tears and wipe their eyes. The onion was frightfully strong.

Mistigris shook his head angrily, and shook it again. The onion smell was getting among his whiskers, and he hated it. Then he stood up.

Dibdin, giving a huge sniff, choking back his tears, bolted through between the cat's front and back legs, hauling the heavy corner of the teacloth after him. It was like pulling the corner of a thick carpet – almost heavier than he could drag.

Hirondel bolted round behind the cat – leaping over his tail – and was there to help his friend pull the cloth halfway through the gap.

"For heaven's sake, girls, take the onion away!" he called. "Or we shan't be able to see what we are doing."

Gulping and gasping the two girls put the onion back together again and wrapped its peel around it. Then they returned it to the vegetable rack.

Mistigris sat down again, twisted his head round, and began to dry his shoulder-blades.

Chanterol seized the rope that was fastened to the corner of the teacloth and clambered back up the table leg. He passed the end of the rope over the cup-hook and dropped it down to his friends below, who fastened it to the opposite corner of the teacloth. Dibdin climbed up with the rope again, which was passed over the cup-hook and the free end dropped down.

"Now we must all pull," said Hirondel.

The girls had returned from the pantry, dodging the tail of the dog Garm (still fast asleep, thank goodness) and tiptoeing past the broom-cupboard where the savage Norn stirred and growled in her dusty corner.

There was a lot of slack rope on the floor, so they all took hold of it – Dibdin, Hirondel, Chanterol, Ilthra, Chraselas, and Prince Coriander. They pulled and pulled and pulled, until the slack was all taken up, and the teacloth began to creep along the floor, under the cat Mistigris, who was now lying on his side, and licking one of his elbows.

He turned his head sharply, as the cloth slipped along the polished floor under his stomach.

"Now we must be ready for one strong, fast pull!" hissed Prince Coriander. "For the cat Mistigris is not going to like it at all when he suddenly feels himself hoisted up into the air. And that will be the worst danger point – before his feet are off the ground, while he is still able to spring at us."

Above, on the kitchen table, and on the shelves, and the counter by the sink, and on every level spot, the kitchen elves were clustered, breathless, watching, all this time.

"Oh, if only my boy hadn't made that silly boast," mourned Mopsa, the mother of Hirondel.

"Oh, if only you hadn't been so sharp with the lad and told him he'd have to go into exile," whispered the queen to King Corodil, and he looked at her crossly.

"Well, it's too late now. I did tell him. You can't plant a daisy once it has been chopped down."

"*One!*" called Prince Coriander. "TWO! THREE!"

All six of them pulled on the rope until their muscles twanged like guitar strings. And the cat Mistigris – to everybody's amazement – suddenly rose six inches in the air; to his own huge astonishment and disgust.

"They've done it, they've done it!" shrieked Mopsa.

"But will they ever be able to get him any higher?" muttered the king doubtfully. For

Mistigris had begun to struggle and kick, and he was slipping backwards in the sling of teacloth that supported him; in another minute he would be out of the sling, and the valiant six who had hoisted him up would be in deadly danger. For Mistigris was looking very angry indeed. No cat likes to be treated with disrespect. His ears were back and his eyes were slits and his whiskers were flattened back against his head.

Then – at that very moment – everybody heard a sound in the garden outside. A loud, wild caterwauling: Morow-wow-wow, wow, wow, wow, *graaaaatch!*

"That's the big white cat from next door," muttered Queen Corasin. "And the yellow striped one from three houses along."

With two rapid kicks, Mistigris got himself out of the sling. He didn't waste a single glance at the elves, but shot across the kitchen, out through his cat-flap, and away.

A long sigh of relief went up from everybody in the kitchen. Except Garm the dog, who was still asleep.

King Corodil said, "Since all four paws of the cat Mistigris were definitely seen to be off the ground, I declare the threat of banishment null and void. The Games will be concluded tomorrow night. It is time that everybody went to bed. But please tidy up all that mess first; otherwise THEY will be sure to notice something."

And he stumped away to his palace.

Coriander, Hirondel, Dibdin, Chanterol, Chraselas, and Ilthra quickly tidied away the rope and bits of onion peel, untied the teacloth, and put it back on the Dutch airer. They had to do this by hauling it up on the rope; it was a long and tiring job. Dawn was breaking by the time they had finished, and so they were obliged to leave the cup-hook. It is still screwed to the underside of the kitchen table. But so far THEY have not noticed this.

"I hope that will cure you of silly bragging," Hirondel's mother said to him.

And Queen Corasin said to her husband, "Don't you think perhaps it is time you retired, dear?"

3 The Nixie's Rescue

"I am going to rescue that poor nixie girl who got taken by the trolls," said Prince Coriander. "That is, if they haven't eaten her already."

"*What?*" shrieked his mother the queen. "How can you go and do a dangerous thing like that, when you have only just come home after so long?"

"I do not consider it *at all* necessary to go and rescue a nixie girl," said King Corodil. "The nixies never do anything for us. They just sit in the sink and sing silly songs and play with the water. Why should we do anything for them?"

"I like their singing," said Prince Coriander. "And they are very sad about their sister. I want to help them."

Off he went to talk to the nixies who live in the sink. They are green all over, and their eyes and hair are golden, and they have voices like liquid moonlight.

"I want to try and rescue your sister from the trolls in the deep-freeze," said Coriander. "Is she still there?"

"Oh yes!" chorused the other four sisters, Watersleep, Watersmoon, Waterswit, and Watersweet. "We can hear her weeping and crying at sunrise and at moonrise. The trolls are keeping her for their great feast on Trolls' Night."

"When is that?"

"When the old moon has gone and before the new moon has come. But how can you possibly rescue her? The trolls are terribly powerful. They could turn you to ice-dust, or chew you up on the spot, or many other terrible things. And there are so many of them – ever so many more than there used to be!"

"How many?"

"We don't exactly know, but many, many," replied the nixies, shivering.

"Do they never leave the deep-freeze?"

"Oh yes, when they go out hunting ghost-deer."

"Then I'll pick a night when they do that, and try to slip in and rescue your sister while they are gone."

"You'll need something to cut through her chains," said the nixies, "for the troll chains are made of ice and fire and no ordinary blade will cut them."

"Where could I find something that will?"

"Well," they said doubtfully, "the old Norn in the broom cupboard, Urd, has a pair of tongs made from light. She uses them to pull out the quills of her porcupine when they grow too long. If you could borrow those . . . But the Norn herself is a very dreadful person, and if she were to lay hold of you in her talons, you'd be done for."

"Well, I will see if I can borrow her tongs," resolved Prince Coriander. And he crossed the kitchen and, quaking a little inside himself but not letting it show, tapped on the door of the broom-cupboard.

"Who's there?" croaked a rusty voice.

"Prince Coriander. I want to ask if I can borrow your tongs."

"What can you do for me in return?" croaked the voice, and suddenly the door flew open. Inside was a cobwebby old lady who looked half witch, half skeleton; she clutched in one of her taloned hands a three-legged broom. At her feet squatted a prickly porcupine. She and the porcupine stared at Prince Coriander as if they would like nothing better than to sink their teeth in him. But he said boldly:

"I can bring you some news of your sister Verd, who lives out in the garden."

"How is my dear sister?" croaked the Norn, looking interested at once. For it is a rule that the three Norns, who are sisters, may never meet. One of them lives in the present, one in the past, and one in the future.

"Your sister Verd is well, and has a trail of green mossy hair down to her ankles. And the birds are building nests on her shoulders."

"Very well," said the Norn, "for that piece of news I shall allow you to borrow my tongs. But you must let me have them back by tomorrow, or I shall send my porcupine to spike you with his prickles." At which Ferd the porcupine rattled his prickles fiercely.

The Norn handed over her tongs, which were made of white light, and Prince Coriander, tucking them under his belt, went in search of his friend Chanterol, who had a little pipe made of clay and shaped like a deer's antler, on which he could play beautiful tunes, and, as well, imitate the noise made by any animal or bird.

"Can you imitate the call of a ghost-deer?" said Prince Coriander.

"Easy!" replied Chanterol, and he blew on his pipe, as hard as he could, and the kitchen filled with a sound like the call of ghost-deer as they run through the woods and over the moors. The dog Garm stirred in his sleep, for it sounded as if there were a whole forestful of them right there, between the china-cupboard and the sink and the gas cooker and the deep-freeze.

By and by Coriander and Chanterol, who had hidden themselves behind the bread bin, heard the voices of trolls inside their lair.

"Come out, brothers, let us go out and hunt! There must be a whole herd of deer passing by. We need more meat for our feast on Trolls' Night."

Soon the door of the deep-freeze opened and a

whole crowd of trolls came trooping out. As soon as
they were outside they began to grow, for trolls can
take any size that is convenient to them. They were
dreadful in appearance, for they gave off blue light,
and deadly cold, and their eyes spun round in their
heads like wheels. At the sight of them the nixies in
the sink dived under water, and even the kelpies in
the dishwasher retired into the Black Pit. The trolls
rushed off, yelling their hunting cry, waving their
spears, after the ghost-deer they hoped to catch and
kill.

Then Prince Coriander bounded up, and opened
the deep-freeze, and leapt inside. There he saw the
poor nixie girl, right at the back, tied down in a

corner by a hundred heavy chains. The trolls could not freeze her, for nixies are cold-blooded to begin with, but they had starved her, and she was so miserable that the sight of Prince Coriander was just another terror.

"Oh, who are you?" she gasped.

"I am Prince Coriander, of the elves, and I have come to rescue you. Keep still." And the prince set to work with old Urd's tongs, pulling apart the chains of ice and fire that held the nixie down. They were riveted to a huge block of ice, and the job was a great deal harder, and took much longer, than he had expected. "Are you Waterslenda?" he asked the green girl, as he tugged and beat at the chains.

The girl nodded. "Oh, please be careful!" she cried. "Don't make such a noise. For they left an old troll guarding me. He is there, in the other corner. If you bang and crash, you are likely to wake him."

Sure enough, in another corner, Prince Coriander could see an old troll, snoring by a fire of red-hot icicles.

"I'll be as quiet as I can," he said. "But I have to work fast, for soon the trolls outside will discover there aren't any ghost-deer, and then they will be coming home again."

One by one the chains dropped off, until there were only three left. But then the prince accidentally touched Waterslenda on the back of her hand with the Norn's tongs.

"Oh!" she shrieked. "That tickles! It's so cold!

It's so hot!'' And she burst into a peal of laughter.

And at that Uggslid, the aged troll who had been left to guard her, woke up and saw Prince Coriander.

"What in the name of all that's trolley are *you*?" he growled, and made for the prince, growing as he went. Prince Coriander knew he must act fast, and he did – he leapt towards the troll, opening the tongs as wide as they would go, seized the troll's nose, gave a tremendous tug, and pulled it off.

A troll cannot survive without his nose – down sank Uggslid, with a clap like a burst balloon, and soon shrank away to nothing at all.

Quickly Prince Coriander turned back to the chains that held Waterslenda, and pulled off the last three. But now he heard a warning shout from his friend Chanterol, who had been left to keep watch outside the deep-freeze. "Look out, prince! Make haste! The trolls are coming back."

What had happened was quite outside the prince's calculations.

In the middle of the dark park the hunting trolls had come across a pair of real ghost-deer and – as bad luck would have it – one of the hunted deer galloped round in a circle and, flying from the trolls, came right into the kitchen where the elves lived. Ghost-deer, of course, can go straight through any walls, doors, or windows, and often do.

Quick as a flash, Prince Coriander pulled the nixie girl out of the trolls' lair. Clasping her in his arms he made a tremendous leap and sprang straight from the deep-freeze to the sink, where her sisters, Watersleep, Watersmoon, Watersweet, and Waterswit, were waiting to welcome her.

"Oh, dearest sister! We thought we'd never see you again."

"Oh, how thin and pale you are!"

"Quick, we must hide from the trolls!"

Faster than light, all five girls sank down in a ribbon of water and vanished from view.

The trolls were still hurtling round and round the kitchen, raging and crackling and giving off blue fumes, in pursuit of the ghost-deer, which managed to keep just two bounds ahead of them.

Old Urd, the Norn, put her head out of her cobwebby cupboard. "What is all this commotion?" she croaked. "How is a person supposed to get any sleep around here?"

And, in a rage, she began laying about her with her three-legged broom, banging the trolls as they passed by. Urd is not afraid of any trolls – in fact she is afraid of nothing at all except her younger sister Swurd.

In the confusion, the ghost-deer managed to escape up the chimney, but the trolls did not notice that.

"Where is it, where is it?" they yelled, and, taking no notice of Urd, they began opening biscuit tins and throwing over chairs and pulling out drawers and creating the most terrible mess and chaos. "Where did the deer go?"

"He went in *there*," maliciously croaked the Norn, and she pointed with one of her long claws to the round lettuce-dryer. Ten – twenty – thirty trolls instantly pulled off the lid and leapt inside, making themselves small enough to do so.

"Now's your chance, prince!" cackled the Norn. "Put the lid back on and *spin*!"

Prince Coriander did not wait to be told twice. He clapped the lid back on the lettuce-dryer and began

to whirl it round, faster and faster, faster and faster. The trolls inside began to scream like gulls, but being whirled round so fast robbed them of their power to grow and made them quite helpless.

Prince Coriander whirled and whirled, until his arm ached, but he dare not stop. The rest of the trolls, hovering in the air or perched on the deep-freeze, were letting out blue flames of rage and looked ready to tear him in pieces, but they, too, dared not touch him while he was whirling their friends inside the dryer. How long can I go on? wondered the prince.

"Best get back to your cave, trolls!" shrieked the Norn. "Sun rises in ninety seconds. If you stay out, my sister Swurd will be after you!"

Then the trolls panicked. True enough, the hunt had lasted so long that outside the windows the sky was turning pink; night was nearly over. And any troll who is outside his cave when the sun rises is immediately turned to stone. All the trolls perched about the kitchen made for the deep-freeze and there was a furious battle just outside the door as they kicked and fought and scuffled to get in. Some managed to squeeze through in time, but there was a terrible chorus of wails and groans abruptly cut short as the sun rose, and the trolls who were left outside changed to blocks of black stone, and dropped heavily on to the floor. And Prince Coriander, feverishly spinning the lid of the lettuce-dryer with an arm that felt ready to come away from its shoulder, heard inside the dryer a series of sharp thuds which meant that the trolls in there, also, had turned to pebbles.

"Well, that's rid the place of a lot of them. But what a mess!" grumbled the Norn, glancing about the untidy kitchen, where tins had been emptied, drawers turned upside down, chairs knocked over, and teacloths tossed on the floor. "You elves had best tidy it up before THEY come down. That's your business. And give me back my tongs, Prince!"

Prince Coriander gratefully gave the Norn her tongs. Then he put two fingers to his mouth and whistled shrilly. Right away, half a hundred elves came dropping out of the china-cupboard, and began busily wiping and sweeping and putting everything to rights.

"We really ought to be given overtime pay – having to work like this in daylight," remarked one of them. "Danger money, too!"

"Stow your row, thickhead!" said another. "Hasn't Prince Coriander got rid of goodness knows how many trolls, who were a danger to the entire kitchen community? You ought to be grateful to him."

Disposing of the trolls on the floor who had turned to stone proved quite an awkward task. In the end the elves solved it by shoving the stones on to sheets of newspaper and then dragging the newspaper out of doors; the stones were left on the pavement, where they puzzled a great many people.

"I want to marry that nixie girl," said Prince Coriander to his father next day.

"*What*? Marry a nixie? Have you gone clean off your head? Elves *never* marry nixies," said King Corodil.

"Why not?"

"Well because – because – because they are different, that's why! Elves are warm-blooded, nixies are cold-blooded. It just wouldn't do. Nixies have *never* married elves."

"She is very beautiful," said Prince Coriander obstinately, "and I love her, and I am going to ask her to marry me."

"If you do," said his father, "I shall disinherit you! My brother Corofin has twenty sons – I shall offer the Elf Crown to one of my twenty nephews."

"Oh, Corodil, you can't do that!" cried his wife anxiously. "Don't you remember that if an Elf King decides to disinherit his son, there has to be a contest, and the crown goes to the winner?"

"Very well; then there will have to be a contest," growled Corodil. "For I'm not leaving the Elf Crown to a besotted boy who wants to marry a green nixie."

"I shall ask her tomorrow," said Prince Coriander. "But," he added sadly, "who knows? Perhaps she won't have me."

4   The Furnace Dragon

"There shall be a contest to decide who is going to be the new King of the Elves," said King Corodil. "I'm getting old and tired. It's time I retired. And it can't be too soon. I don't feel a bit well."

He coughed and the queen looked at him anxiously, for he had never said such a thing before.

"But why can't our dear son Coriander be king?"

"Because the young idiot wants to marry a nixie. Imagine a nixie as Queen of the Elves? No," said the king firmly, "I shall hold a contest among all my nephews."

"You can't stop Coriander from going in for the contest. That would be against elf law."

"No. But I daresay he won't win. After all, I have twenty nephews."

However, when the terms of the contest were announced, only two of the twenty nephews were able to apply. It turned out that twelve of the rest

were still under fifteen, so they were not eligible.
And, of the other six, four were doing their naval
service, and one was in prison for stealing a horse.

So the contenders for the kingship were Prince
Coriander and his two cousins, Borodig and Finpair.

Borodig was a fat, cheerful boy, not very bright. Coriander liked him, but couldn't honestly feel that he would make a very good Elf King, defending his subjects against all the perils they have to live with: trolls, witches, dragons, kelpies, and savage dogs and cats.

Finpair was thin and quiet and rather sly-looking; Prince Coriander knew nothing against him except that, many years ago when they were both boys, Finpair had stolen a pair of Coriander's magic skates and then said he hadn't. But that was a long time in the past. By now he was probably a very good sort of fellow.

"The terms of the contest are this," said King Corodil. "I shall set each of you a task. The one who completes his task first and best will win ten points. The second and third get five points and one point respectively. Then there will be a running race, again for ten, five, and one points. Then you will each have to make some suggestion for a Good Idea. Another ten points. And the one who does best will become king. I shall resign."

Finpair, who had brightened at the sound of the race, for he was a very fast runner, looked a bit thoughtful at the Good Idea. Borodig became very downcast.

"Good Idea?" he mumbled. "How shall I ever think of one?"

"These are the tasks," said King Corodil. "My son Coriander must go to the cellar, subdue the

Furnace dragon, and bring back the silver apples from the apple tree that grows there."

All the listeners gasped with horror. For the Furnace dragon was the most dangerous peril the elves have to face. No one – *no one* ever went into the cellar unless it was a matter of life and death. And then generally it proved a matter of death.

"Oh, Corodil!" wailed the queen.

But the king said grandly: "It is right that my son should have the most dangerous task."

The other tasks were almost as bad, however. Finpair had to climb into the dishwasher, braving the horrible kelpies who live in its slimy depths, and rescue Queen Corasin's ring, which had once accidentally been left lying in a salt-cellar and tossed in by one of THEM.

Hearing this announcement, Finpair looked first thoughtful, then surprisingly confident.

Borodig's task was to climb into the refrigerator (braving the young trolls who go to school in that place) and bring back a supply of jam turnover, which was King Corodil's favourite food. "How shall I ever do that?" he wailed despondently.

"I'll help you!" whispered Finpair. "Anything to keep out Coriander!"

The prince was not paying attention to the other two contestants. He wandered off, deep in thought, to ask the advice of the Norn in the broom-cupboard, who had helped him once before. That evening he knocked on her cupboard door.

"Who's there?" she snarled.

"It's I, Prince Coriander. I want to ask your advice. I have brought you a leaf covered with runes from your sister Verd."

The Norn opened her cobwebby door, looked at the leaf, sniffed it, ate it, and then demanded, "What's the trouble this time, Prince? What do you want?"

"I have to go to the cellar, and subdue the Furnace dragon, and bring back the silver apples."

"The Furnace dragon! What next? How long do you expect to live? Well," said the Norn, "you will need to use cunning there. You can't overcome him by force."

"Oh?" said the prince, disappointed. "I hoped I could kill him and then we'd never have to fear him again."

"No, no, you can't do that. There will always be a Furnace dragon. You must ask him a riddle. And while he's trying to think of the answer, be picking your apples. You must take an ash flower with you, so that the sweet scent will make the dragon drowsy. Otherwise he would probably swallow you before you can even ask your riddle."

"Where do I find an ash flower?"

"Growing out of the hearth stone at moonrise," said the Norn. "Now don't bother me any more, I'm tired. Mind you take care to pick *all* the silver apples. That's important."

"Why?"

But she had gone in and closed the door.

Though the prince didn't know it, Finpair and Borodig had hidden behind a dustpan and listened to this conversation. Finpair thought it would be worth his while to learn Coriander's plans.

"It's a good thing we listened," he told Borodig. "You can pick one of those ash flowers too, and use it to put the troll children to sleep while you take a

piece of jam turnover. Take a good big piece," he suggested craftily, knowing how greedy Borodig was, "and then you and I can have a bit of it before you take the rest to the king."

Prince Coriander went to the hearth stone at moonrise and picked one of the nine great white flowers that suddenly sprang up in bloom, straight out of the stone. The flower smelt sweet as honey, and drowsy too; it made the prince yawn, as he walked along.

"This won't do," he thought, and he strapped it on his back, where the scent would drift off behind him as he walked along.

Then he climbed down into the cellar, which took him two days of hard travel in the dark. He had a glow worm to light his way, but even so the dark was dreadful. Lower and lower he climbed, down the stone stairs, and at last he could see the dragon's eye glow red, and hear its snoring breath.

Then there was a loud huffing roar, as the dragon smelt him and heard him and came to sudden life; it spread open black steel wings, and shot out a fearful claw. But Prince Coriander, waving the ash flower in front of him until its sweet scent spread over the cellar, called out:

"Purple yellow red and green
  The king can't touch me nor the queen
  See me wet, see me dry
  Who can tie a bow in the sky?"

The Furnace dragon can never resist riddles. He
began to think about this one, wrinkling his
cast-iron forehead, grinding his aluminium teeth.

"See me wet, see me dry," he mumbled and
muttered to himself.

Meanwhile Prince Coriander, without wasting a
moment, sprang across, past the dragon and his
furnace, to the far corner of the cellar where a tiny
apple tree could be seen; there were the silver

apples, which were the size of currants, gleaming faintly in the light of the dragon's red eye.

The prince had brought a silk bag tied to his belt. He picked the apples and packed them into the bag with feverish speed. The ash flower began to droop and wilt in the dragon's fiery heat; anyway, ash flowers last for only three days.

Having picked all the apples – or he *thought* he had picked them all – Prince Coriander scampered back up the steps, taking them in terrific grasshopper leaps. Only just in time . . .

"I give up!" roared the dragon. "What's the answer?"

"A rainbow!" called the prince, and then he flung himself through the cellar door, just before a blast of white-hot heat followed him. One of his heels was badly singed, and the ash flower turned to silver cinders.

When Coriander returned to the palace, he found that the other two competitors had arrived before him. Borodig had brought an enormous piece of jam turnover. It would have been bigger still, but he had stopped on the way to eat half himself. And he would have come sooner still, but his greedy feast had made him fall asleep for a day and a night. So Finpair had arrived first with his gold ring.

"It was a dreadful business fighting off those unpleasant kelpies," he said modestly. "But the thought of your majesty's pleasure at getting the ring back spurred me on."

"Oh, my dear, dear ring!" cried Queen Corasin. "It has my name engraved inside it, just as I remember. And a good-luck rune. Oh, how pleased I am to get it back."

King Corodil was busily eating the rest of the jam turnover. It was his favourite food. So Prince Coriander's bag of silver apples did not cause much excitement. The bag was put on a shelf, and the king said, "Tomorrow we will hold the running race and the rest of the contest."

However in the middle of the night King Corodil had such terrible pains that the queen became seriously alarmed.

"Oh, I shall die, I shall die!" he groaned. "I shall

die before my successor has been appointed."

The queen sent a palace page running for the doctor, who had trained for five years under Urd the Norn, and was very wise. He said at once: "The king has been eating much too much jam turnover. I can tell that from the colour of his eyes. He is gravely ill and may even die. I'm afraid the remedy is a difficult one: he needs apple-sauce made from the silver apples that grow in the cellar."

"Oh, but that is no problem at all!" cried the queen joyously. "For my dear son Coriander has just brought a whole bagful."

"Did he pick the whole crop?"

"Yes, every one."

"Then that should just save the king."

So the silver apples were made into apple-sauce, and the king swallowed it, and began to feel a little, just a *little* better. But still he was not quite better.

But before this the queen, stirring the apple-sauce, had made a shocking discovery. She was very startled to hear the gold ring, when it grew warm in the steam, let out a little golden cry:

> "I'm not your true ring
> You can hear when I sing!
> The rune, the rune,
> Doesn't sing the right tune."

The queen took off her ring and looked inside. There were her initials, but she realised that the rune inscribed on the gold was not the right one. In fact the ring was just a cunning imitation – not her own ring at all!

She hated to tell the king this when he was so ill. He was still very far from recovery. So she waited.

In the end they had to fetch in the Norn, who came very unwillingly, clattering along on her cobwebby three-legged broom. She took one look at the king, and said: "One of the apples must have been missing. The apple-sauce wasn't strong enough. That prince of yours will have to go back to the cellar for the other apple."

"Oh, my goodness!" wept the queen. "It will be *much* more dangerous this time!"

"Can't help that," grunted the Norn. "He should have picked all the apples in the first place." And she retired to her broom-cupboard.

Prince Coriander went back to the hearth stone at moonrise and picked another ash flower. And he climbed down into the cellar again. He did it faster this time, for he knew the way, but still it took a long time and he was very worried about his poor old father, lying so ill. Suppose the king should die before Coriander got back? And it will all be my fault, he thought, for not making sure that I had picked all the apples. What a fool I was!

It took more courage to go back the second time.

"Who's there?" roared the dragon, flashing his red eye.

The prince waved his ash flower, and quickly shouted:

"A tree in my head, I'm ready to fall
   Once I was a blossom and now I'm a ball."

This was all that came into his head, which happened to be full of apples at that moment.

But the dragon, who had never eaten an apple in his life, was wholly puzzled by the riddle.

"A tree in my head? What can that be? A fossil?"

Prince Coriander dashed across the cellar floor, found the last apple, a tiny, misshaped one growing low down near the ground, picked it, and sprang away, faster than a cricket.

"Wait, wait!" roared the dragon, as he bounded up the steps. "What has a tree in its head?"

"An apple!" called the prince, just before he nipped through the door.

A hot blast of fire followed him, and burned his other heel, so that he was limping badly by the time he returned to the palace.

The lost apple was speedily made into apple-sauce and administered to the king, who swallowed it down, sat up in bed, and declared that he was better.

"Now we will hold the running race!" he announced.

Prince Coriander's heart sank. He was so lame, with two badly burned heels, that he knew he did not stand a chance against the fast Finpair.

But now Queen Corasin spoke up. "I'm sorry to tell your majesty," she said to her husband, "but your nephew Finpair is a nasty cheat! He had a ring made which *looks* exactly like the one I lost. But it is not my ring and I can prove it."

She called for a boiling kettle, and held the ring in the steam. And again it sang its little song:

> "I'm not your true ring
>   You can tell when I sing
>   The rune, the rune
>   Doesn't sing the right tune."

"Good heavens!" said the king, greatly shocked. "To think that a nephew of mine should stoop to such a low trick!"

Finpair was summoned, and came to the palace all smiles. He knew that Prince Coriander was very lame, and he knew he could run much faster than Borodig; he thought that he was certain to be appointed king.

But he met with a very different reception from the one he expected.

"You are a vulgar, cheating swindler, sir! To think that such a person had the impertinence to believe he might become King of the Elves! I hereby sentence you to a hundred years of exile, to be passed in the windy Snow-country south of Nowhere."

"You haven't got your crown on, dear," whispered the queen.

The king glared at her, clapped his crown on his head, and repeated, "I sentence you, Finpair, to a hundred years of exile in the windy Snow-country south of Nowhere."

The fact that King Corodil said the words with the crown on his head made them absolute law. Finpair was obliged to leave the palace, very crushed and crestfallen, saddle a horse, and depart for the windy Snow-country.

"Now we'll hold the running race," said the king.

"That is unfair!" said the queen. "Poor Coriander has two dreadfully singed heels."

"The race must be held today," said the king obstinately.

But when it came to the race, fat Borodig was still so slowed down by the enormous greedy quantity of jam turnover he had eaten, that, in spite of his burns, the prince was able to win the race quite easily.

"Now you both have to think of a Good Idea," said the king. "Both competitors are equal at the moment, since Borodig brought in his jam turnover long before Coriander arrived with the bag of apples – which, anyway, was missing one."

"And a lot of good that jam turnover did you!" snapped the queen. "It nearly killed you. If Coriander hadn't brought the apples, you wouldn't be here now."

"Hush, woman!" said the king. "Borodig, let's hear your Good Idea."

Poor Borodig looked this way. He looked that way. He rubbed his forehead. He squeezed his cheeks. He racked his brains. But not a single Good Idea could he produce.

"Well, Coriander," said the king at last, "what's yours?"

"My Good Idea," said Coriander, "is that I should have a try at getting mother's ring out of the dishwasher."

"Oh yes!" cried the queen clapping her hands, "Oh yes, that's a perfectly splendid idea."

King Corodil was obliged to admit that his son had won the contest, and Coriander was proclaimed Heir Apparent of the Elves.

"But," said the king, "I feel so much better now that I don't think I shall retire just yet after all."

Borodig was hugely relieved that he didn't have to be king. "Coriander will do it much better. He is a very good fellow. If you ask me, being king is too much like hard work!"

5   The Kelpies' Bowl

"How can I get mother's ring out of the dishwasher?" wondered Prince Coriander.

Down at the bottom of the dishwasher live the kelpies. When the tide rises high, up they come; you can hear them booming and wailing and thrashing about inside. Kelpies are dreadful beings: they look like huge horses, with the heads of cows, they have enormous quantities of dagger-sharp teeth, their hides are covered with shells and weed, they have long claws, curved and sharp as grass-hooks, and they also have savage and unpleasant natures. Moreover, although they can and often do make a great deal of noise, laughing and whistling and wailing, they can also be as silent as fog, creeping along behind people and snatching them unexpectedly.

Kelpies, of course, only come out at night. But the elves only come out at night too.

"You will certainly need a rowan twig," said Coriander's mother Queen Corasin. "That much I do know. Kelpies have a great dislike of rowan twigs."

A rowan twig didn't seem a lot of help against huge savage kelpies, with skins thicker than rhinoceros hide and teeth like the alps. But still, Prince Coriander paid a visit to his cousins, the Garden Elves, and came back with a bundle of twigs. He gave some to his mother to keep in the palace. "Just in case the kelpies chase me home."

Queen Corasin began to worry. "Oh dear, oh dear, I wish you'd never said you'd go after that wretched ring. Why can't it stay where it is, at the bottom of the dishwasher?"

But King Corodil said, "The boy certainly can't be king until he has done one or two things like that. Why, at his age, I had performed all sorts of brave deeds: beaten off the Larder Goblins, and defeated the Garbage Ghosts, and fought a hand-to-hand combat with the Nametape Monster, and rescued you, my love, from the Sewing-machine ogre."

"Very true," said the queen, drying her eyes. "Well, Coriander is a brave boy. And I'm sure he'll do his best to recover the ring."

"We'll hold a feast to welcome him when he gets back," said King Corodil, who loved feasts. "We'll have honey-cakes and frumenty and ambrosia-bread, and metheglin, and red-hot mead. You had better get the palace girls to work, making the honey-cakes and ambrosia, and I'll start the lads

heating up the red-hot mead.''

Off he bustled to set about this. The queen looked after him anxiously. She thought it was much too soon to begin arranging for such celebrations. And she knew a thing that would have made King Corodil furious if he had known it too: Prince Coriander had gone off to consult his friends the nixie girls who live in the sink. He thought they might have useful advice to offer about how to deal with kelpies, for nixies and kelpies both live in the water, and, indeed, when the kelpies can't think of any other harm to do, and if the tides are right, they sometimes climb out of the dishwasher and give the nixies a great deal of trouble.

Prince Coriander found his friends laughing and dancing and plaiting their golden hair in the long winding ribbon of water that comes down from the tap into the kitchen sink. The nixies are green, with golden eyes and hair, and they have beautiful voices and fun-loving natures.

"There you are, prince!" they called, laughing and splashing. "Come and play with us! Come and sing with us!"

There were five of them, sisters: Waterslenda, Watersleep, Watersmoon, Waterswit and Watersweet. They were all very fond of the prince, but Waterslenda loved him best, for he had rescued her from the trolls in the deep-freeze.

"I can't play with you today, dear friends," he said, "for I have promised to try and get back my mother's ring, which lies at the bottom of the dishwasher."

At this the sisters looked very grave.

"You will be in horrible danger! If the kelpies catch you, they will munch you up like a sardine! The ring has been there such a long time – why not leave it?"

"My mother misses it. It is a magic ring, which prevents her from feeling any aches or pains. And, now she is growing older, she needs it more."

The nixies never feel any aches or pains, so they found this hard to understand.

But Waterslenda said, "Well, if you must go, you must. You will have to wait until low tide, for you can't get into the dishwasher except at low tide."

"How do I get in then?"

"Climb or jump up to the top, and press the red button. Then the side of the dishwasher will open."

"What must I do next?"

"Climb inside. Mind you take a rowan twig with you! That will stop the kelpies from smelling you. At low tide they are all down out of sight, lurking in the Black Pot Pipe."

"What is the Black Pot Pipe?"

"That's where the kelpies lurk at low tide," said Waterswit rather crossly. "Really, prince, you are very slow!"

"Then," went on Watersleep, "you must climb down through the prongs of the dishwasher. Mind you do not fall! It is a giddy and dangerous height. You had better tie a rope round your waist and fasten one end of it to the prongs up at the top."

This sounded like excellent advice to the prince,

who resolved to get a long rope made of human hair.

"The kelpies sleep very lightly. The softest sound will wake them."

"Will they come out at low tide?"

"Oh yes, they may. But what they can also do is switch on the dishwasher, so that the tide may come flooding in. Are you a good swimmer, prince?"

"Middling," said the prince, who could not swim very well, and was beginning to look more and more discouraged.

"Well, if you are only middling, you had best wear a life jacket, for the water may come flooding in faster than I can say these words."

Rope, life jacket, wrote the prince on his tablets.

"What if the kelpies come after me?" he asked.

"If they do, you are probably doomed – unless you can stab each kelpie with a red-hot wimble."

"A wimble? What is a wimble?"

"Really, you are ignorant! A gimlet – an awl – a corkscrew."

Prince Coriander sighed. "I can't very well carry a red-hot corkscrew with me into the dishwasher. It would have cooled off before I ever climbed down to the bottom. Isn't there anything else I can do?"

"Yes," said Watersweet. "You can break the kelpies' pearl bowl."

"Pearl bowl?"

"It is their greatest treasure. At spring tides they drink salt wine out of it. Queen Thetis gave it to their great-grandfather."

"Where do they keep the pearl bowl?"

"Down at the bottom."

Something to smash pearl bowl, wrote Coriander on his tablets. Then he thanked the sisters kindly, bade them goodbye, and left them to their dancing.

"You should have told him not to take any piece of the pearl bowl away with him," pointed out Watersmoon.

"The prince is a gentleman. He would never steal anything, even a piece of the kelpies' bowl," said Waterslenda indignantly.

"You think too much of that boy!" scolded her sisters. "He is extremely ignorant, he can hardly swim, and he isn't even cold-blooded. Put him out of your mind. A nixie can't possibly marry an elf."

"But I love him!" sighed Waterslenda.

Meanwhile Prince Coriander supplied himself with a long, long rope, a small hammer, a large piece of cork, which he strapped to his chest, and a bunch of rowan twigs, which he stuck in his hair.

Thus equipped, he sprang to the top of the dishwasher and pressed the red button.

Tide was at its lowest, and the whole side of the dishwasher slowly leaned outwards, showing a forest of white hooks and racks inside, arranged in layers, going right the way down to the bottom, which was dark and green and damp. A channel led to the Black Pot Pipe. Far, far down, Prince Coriander could see something white and gleaming and circular. That must be the kelpie's pearl bowl,

he thought. And inside that, he could see something that shone even brighter – a tiny twinkle of gold.

That must be my dear mother's magic ring, he thought.

The height made him dizzy. But he set his teeth, and tied one end of his rope firmly to one of the topmost prongs, and then began doggedly climbing down, hand over hand, paying out the rope as he went, sometimes twisting a length of it round a prong, letting himself carefully down from one rack to another.

It was a long, slow climb. Oh, if only the kelpies don't hear me, he thought. He tried to be as quiet as a cloud. And he wondered how long it would be before the tide began coming in again.

It was hot and damp and steamy and silent inside the dishwasher. And it felt very dangerous indeed – even more dangerous than it had in the trolls' lair, or the Utility Desert, or the cellar where the Furnace dragon lived.

But at last Prince Coriander was down on the bottom rack of all, and not far away he saw the beautiful pearl bowl of the kelpies, standing right way up. It was so large that twenty elves could have sat in it, and it shone like the full moon. It had been carved out of a single pearl.

In the middle lay Queen Corasin's ring.

Prince Coriander took off his shoes, and, in his sock-feet, stepped delicately into the bowl. He tiptoed over the shining, slippery surface, and

grabbed the ring, which he pushed on to his finger.

As he did so, he was horrified to hear a deep, deep groan. That was one of the kelpies waking from sleep. Then he heard a wild watery laugh. That was another kelpie waking. Then, in a chorus, all the kelpies began laughing and whistling and wailing until the sound was louder than ten gales at sea, all blowing at the same time.

Prince Coriander leapt for the side of the pearl bowl. But, in his sock-feet, he slipped, and fell headlong. He already had in his hand the hammer which he had pulled out of his pocket; the hammer hit the pearl bowl and smashed it into fifty pieces. Prince Coriander fell through, right down to the bottom of the dishwasher, right beside the entrance to the Black Pot Pipe.

And, coming out of the Black Pot Pipe, he saw the dreadful whiskery face, and the huge staring eyes, and the horns, and gaping mouth, and sharklike teeth of a kelpie. Behind the first kelpie were others – two, ten, twenty, fifty.

"Mercy on me!" gasped the prince. Luckily the kelpies are slow; they passed right by him. And luckily also the rope was still tied to his waist, and the upper end of the rope still firmly fastened above; the prince began pulling himself up with frantic speed, hand over hand, clutching the rope with his hands, and with his feet and legs crossed, as sailors do, and he thanked the stars that he had spent a year at sea and knew how to climb ropes.

At first the kelpies were too startled by the sight of their broken bowl to pay attention to anything else. They did not notice Prince Coriander in the darkness above their heads, climbing, climbing up his rope.

"Our bowl, our bowl, our beautiful bowl! How can it have broken? It was not very old, only a thousand years. Can a stone have fallen on to it?"

They began trundling about in the bottom of the dishwasher, picking up the pearly fragments and trying to fit them together.

But then, as bad luck would have it, one kelpie found the hammer which had shot from the prince's hand as he fell.

"A hammer! Some thief has been in here."

Then they noticed the rope dangling and twitching, and they looked up, and saw Prince Coriander far, far above them, climbing as if his life depended on his speed – which indeed it did.

"Shut the door!" roared the Great Kelpie. "Let the tide flow in!"

Back swished the tide through the Black Pot Pipe – flowing in, faster and faster, swirling up through all the racks of the dishwasher. The prince did not dare look behind him, there was no time for that. But he could hear the water below him, rushing and gurgling.

And one of the kelpies came bounding up after him, leaping from rack to rack, like something halfway between a seal and a gorilla, but much

faster than either. It shot out a terrible taloned paw, and made a grab for the prince.

I'm done for, he thought. But fortunately the kelpie's claw only caught the prince's cork life-jacket, which came off and fell into the water. The prince went on climbing.

Now another kelpie, up at the top of the dishwasher, tried to shut the door. If he had managed to do that, the prince really would have been done for. He would never have escaped. But fortunately the long rope had become tangled and snarled and the bottom end of it was jammed in the hinges. So the door would not shut.

With one last despairing leap the prince hurled himself through the narrowing crack, and was outside the dishwasher.

"Oh, *well done!*" shouted the nixie sisters, who were perched on the taps, and on the edge of the sink, watching to see what happened.

But the prince was not safe yet.

First, a great torrent of water came raging out of the dishwasher after him, right across the kitchen floor.

But he managed to spring to safety, not a moment too soon, on to the kitchen table.

Still he was not safe.

For, though he did not know it, a small piece of the pearl bowl had lodged in his hair, among the rowan twigs. Though he had not meant to steal it, there it was. And so long as he had that on him, the

Great Kelpie could follow him, and did so, churning through the frothy water, all horned and dripping and covered with shells, and his teeth gleaming like the points of daggers.

I'm done for, thought the prince again. And I must not lead this monster towards the palace, because then all the other elves will be done for too.

But, very fortunately, at this moment Queen Corasin happened to be looking out of the palace door, and she saw her son being chased by a terrible water-monster.

"Quick!" shrieked the nixies to the queen. "A red-hot wimble! You must get a red-hot wimble to stab the kelpie!"

Queen Corasin was very quick-witted. Faster than thought she rushed into the palace, wrapped her hands in the king's best mole-fur mantle, and grabbed the red-hot corkscrew which was lying in the fire, heating up, ready to open the great golden flagon of red-hot mead, which was being prepared for the celebration feast.

Clutching the wimble, Queen Corasin ran back to the palace door.

"Hi!" shouted the king after her crossly. "What in the world do you think you are doing?"

But Queen Corasin pushed the wimble, mole-fur cloak and all, into the hands of her son as he came racing up the palace steps, and he turned and thrust it, twirling it as he did so, into the heart of the dreadful Great Kelpie.

And the Great Kelpie groaned and died on the spot, flopping and flapping down the palace steps in a cloud of steam.

"Thanks, Ma!" panted the prince. "I'd surely have been a goner if you hadn't come out just then." And then he said, "Here's your ring back," and slipped the ring off his finger and on to that of the queen.

"Now I'm going to talk to that nixie girl and ask her to marry me," he said.

But when he reached the sink, Waterslenda said, "No, prince. I have been thinking it over, and I think my sisters are right. You could never marry a nixie. You can hardly swim! And I should hate to live in a palace. No, things are better as they are. You must marry some elf girl. But we will always be dear friends."

And so she sent him back to the palace, where all the elves were waiting to welcome him, and to eat ambrosia and honey-cakes and drink red-hot mead.